THE DRAGON CHARMER

Elynne is the daughter of a dragon charmer and desperately wants to help her father in his work but she is a shy girl, easily frightened and the ferocious creatures terrify her. However, when a rare royal dragon – a Crimson Queen – flies into Elynne's life and gives birth to a male baby dragon, there seems to be some kind of strange connection between the baby prince and the girl. When it becomes clear that the baby dragon is in mortal danger, Elynne wonders if she will find the courage to protect him.

A marvellous fantasy from a master of the genre.

OTHER BOOKS BY DOUGLAS HILL

DOUGLAS HILL

The Dragon Charmer

ILLUSTRATED BY PETER MELNYCZUK

BARN OWL BOOKS

The Dragon Charmer was first published
by Hodder Children's Books in 1997
This edition was first published 2004 by Barn Owl Books
157 Fortis Green Road, London N10 3LX
Barn Owl Books are distributed by Frances Lincoln
4 Torriano Mews, Torriano Avenue, London NW5 2RZ

Text copyright © 1997 and 2004 Douglas Hill
Illustrations and cover copyright © 1997 and 2004 Peter Melnyczuk

ISBN 1-903015-36-7

Designed and typeset by Douglas Martin
Printed in China

CONTENTS

For Eugenie and Claire
who could probably charm them too

Chapter One

EMPTY SKIES

Elynne stood on the top of the ridge, waist-deep in coarse grass tangled with shrubs, staring up at the cloudy autumn sky, thinking one thought over and over like a chant. Let this be the day, she was thinking. Let them come today.

In front of her, the slope dropped down to a low area like a natural basin, with the ridge running all around it. Some grass and shrubs grew in the basin, but most of it was bare sand, with a small pool near the centre formed by a spring.

Behind her, on the ridge's other, gentler slope, stood several buildings like long wooden sheds with thatched roofs and, instead of windows, a narrow slit-like opening all the way across the front. The buildings were placed so that each roof rose only slightly above the top of the ridge, the thatch blending in with the grass and brush. Anyone inside, looking out of the window-slits, would have a perfect view of the basin below.

From the buildings a path ran down, across a meadow, towards a farmstead with house, barn, small paddock. And above the gate, which led out to a dirt road, hung a brightly painted sign that read

'DAN DANNEBY
DRAGON CHARMER'

But Elynne wasn't looking at any of that. On the ridge-top, she kept her gaze on the clouds, where occasional breaks showed teasing patches of warm blue. And she kept up her silent chant that was almost a prayer. Let it be today. Let this be the day the dragons come.

Behind her a man's chuckling voice made her jump. 'You won't bring them any sooner by

wishing, Lynnie.'

As she began to turn, a second voice spoke, in a sneering tone. 'Maybe she's aimin' to head north an' look for 'em?'

Elynne turned to face the two men. She was a small, slim girl in a light dress, looking delicate and out of place in the harsh tangle of brush. With her heart-shaped face and big brown eyes, people often said that she looked like a fawn or a kitten. They also said that she looked much younger than her actual age of almost twelve – perhaps because she was mostly quiet and timid.

'I don't think it's funny,' she told the men. 'They're very late. What if . . . what if they don't come at all?'

The tall, curly-haired man with a cheerful face – her father, Dan Danneby – chuckled again. 'They've been late before, sweetheart. It's just because the warm weather's lasted so long. They'll come.'

The other – a bony, ill-tempered man who was Dan's assistant, Niys Vennor – sneered. 'You'd think she'd be glad if they didn't, they scare her so much.'

Elynne flinched. It was true, of course – they *did* scare her. And she knew her fear was a great disappointment to her father, though he had never told her so. Certainly Vennor never missed a chance to taunt her.

'Never mind that, Niys,' Dan said sternly. 'Let's get to work. That shutter needs fixing before they *do* get here.'

Vennor sniffed sourly as the two men moved away to the nearest of the long sheds. 'The girl's got a point, though, Dan, like I keep tryin' to say. We depend on them beasts comin'. An' if they ever start goin' another way or stoppin' somewheres else – we'll be *finished*.'

'Are you singing that old song again?' Dan said lightly.

'Tryin' to make you see sense', Vennor grumbled. 'Catch a bunch of 'em an' keep 'em, I'd say. Put on a show whenever you want. No more worries.'

Dan shook his head. 'Give it a rest, Niys. I'm not in the business of catching dragons. I've told you time and again – people come to see dragons that are wild and beautiful and *free*. Not sad, broken-spirited creatures in cages.'

Vennor grunted, curling his lip again. 'Yeah, yeah. But if this is the time your wild, free dragons don't show up at all, remember I warned you.'

Their voices faded as they entered the shed, where one of the long shutters – which could be lowered protectively over the window-slit – needed repairs. And Elynne sighed unhappily as she went back to her ridge-top vigil. She didn't like agreeing with Vennor, but she had to do so. No matter how afraid she might be, she knew that their livelihood depended on the regular arrival, every spring and autumn, into the basin below her, of hordes of dragons.

Unhappily, she looked out again across the expanse of the valley. Known as the Woodfern Valley, it was wide and richly fertile, with big farms, small farmsteads and scattered villages and towns. And all around the valley, like the battlements of a fortress, stood ranges of hills and mountains.

Westward, the Oldstone Heights were gentle uplands, rounded and softened by age and greenery. To the east, the Raketooth Hills rose higher and stonier, with stark slopes and cliffs of bare rock. Far to the south stood the Cloudtower range, its peaks veiled in mist nearly all the year.

And almost as far away, northward, loomed the mightiest range of all – the Spearcrag, bleak and grim and fierce, its stone spires armoured in snow and ice.

Elynne shivered despite the day's warmth as she stared at the mountains, thinking of the creatures – also fierce and armoured – that lived among those peaks for half of every year. And then the two men emerged from the shed, still arguing.

'Say what you like, Dan Danneby,' Niys Vennor was snarling as she turned to look. 'You can't tell me you wouldn't make yourself *rich* if you had dragons on show all year round.'

Dan shook his head angrily. 'We're doing just fine, now. If you're so keen on being *rich*, Niys, why don't you go and see if you can do better on your own?'

Elynne stifled a laugh. Niys Vennor had only a very *weak* talent, compared to Dan's. He knew he could never succeed on his own as a dragon charmer – and he bitterly resented it.

Although, she thought, her laughter fading, having even a weak ability would be better than not being able to do it at all.

The men were looking up at her, Vennor with a glower, Dan with a small smile. But then their expressions changed and Elynne's thoughts vanished.

They all heard, far away but unmistakeable, a scream – high, piercing, nerve-grindingly harsh. A dragon's scream, as chilling and eerie as the howl of mountain winds.

And as Elynne whirled round, she saw that one of the bright openings in the clouds above them was alive with dragon wings.

Chapter Two

UNKIND WORDS

Elynne sprinted away down the slope and across the meadow, leaving the men behind, flying across the yard to burst through the farmhouse door.

'Aunt, aunt!' she shrieked. 'They're coming, they're *coming!*'

Startled, her Aunt Pedda looked around from the kitchen counter. 'All right, child,' she said briskly. 'No need to shout.'

Pedda was an energetic, grey-haired woman who had come to live with them after Elynne's mother had died when Elynne was just a baby. She and Elynne hurried to the door, peering upward. And they were joined by Old Gidge, the skinny, white-haired 'man of all work', also staring at the sky.

'Ain't many of 'em,' the old man remarked, shading his eyes.

Elynne's delight faded a little. The sky had seemed full of dark wings – but as the dragons drew closer it was clear that there were only about a dozen.

'This'll just be the first lot,' Pedda told her. 'You know how they do – fly in separate bunches.'

Elynne nodded. At least there'll be *some*, she thought. So there can be a show.

Dragons, of course, had been flying out of the northern mountains, in autumn, for as long as anyone in the Woodfern Valley could remember. It was an annual migration, when the dragons flew south for the winter and north again for the summer, just as many sorts of birds did. But, unlike birds, dragons were not made to be airborne for long periods of time. So, on their way from the Spearcrag range to their summer home in the Cloudtowers, and on their way back in spring, the migrating dragons stopped for a rest.

[18]

And – also for as long as anyone could remember – their preferred resting-place had been the sandy basin near the Danneby farmstead.

Indeed, Elynne's father had settled there for just that reason. Because his profession depended on being near the resting dragons.

Dan and Vennor had begun moving the horses – and one small brown donkey – from the paddock to the barn, where they wouldn't be afraid or in danger.

'Gidge!' Dan called. 'Get Donnie, will you?'

'I'll get him!' Elynne cried, and dashed towards the paddock. Donnie the donkey did some work around the place, but he was mostly Elynne's pet. He nuzzled at her in friendly greeting, hoping for a lump of sugar, then trotted along uncomplainingly as she led him to the barn.

Inside, Vennor took the little donkey from her, jerking him along roughly, tying him in a stall. Elynne wanted to tell him off for the roughness, but her father was at the other end of the barn and she didn't have the nerve.

'We should leave *you* in here, too,' Vennor said to her with a nasty grin. 'So the dragons won't scare you to death.'

It was the sort of cruel, mocking thing that he often said to her, and as usual she had no ready answer. She simply walked out of the barn, to rejoin Aunt Pedda and Gidge. And when Dan and Vennor came out they all remained quiet, gathered in the yard, waiting for the dragons to arrive.

But for Elynne the excitement had been spoiled. She was angry at Vennor's unkind mockery, but she was at least as angry at her own response. Or lack of one. She wished, as she had wished for a long time, that she could somehow become brave. To give Niys Vennor a piece of her mind — but above all to be with her father when the dragons came. She wanted that more than anything, and she knew that her father did too. But she also knew, hopelessly, that there was little chance of it. Dan was sure that she had some of the dragon-charming power, but she was just as sure that she would never be able to *use* it. Because the idea of being close to the ferocious creatures simply paralysed her with terror.

Her father tried to tell her that it didn't matter, and Aunt Pedda tried to tell her that there was no shame in being afraid of dragons, and that anyway there had never *been* a girl dragon charmer. But none of that did any good. And Elynne didn't need Vennor to twist the knife with cruel jeering. She could heap a crushing weight of misery and shame on herself without any help – in the wretched knowledge that she would always be a disappointment to her father, and to herself.

And the wretchedness rose in her again as she was unable to stop herself from shrinking, hearing Vennor's snicker, when the group of dragons at last swooped down on leathery wings to settle – beyond the ridge with its half-hidden sheds, into the empty, waiting basin that was their resting-place.

'Right!' Dan said, grinning happily. 'That's a start, anyway.' He turned his grin on to Vennor. 'Just remember, Niys – if we did things your

way, with dragons in cages, we'd have to spend money on *advertising*. This way the dragons do it for us, free.'

Vennor grunted and moved away without replying. And Elynne went with Aunt Pedda to start the preparations.

By then, she knew, word would be spreading, as people reported seeing the first of the dragon arrivals overhead. All over the valley, and in some neighbouring valleys, huge numbers of people would be getting ready to travel to the Danneby farmstead, to see the resting dragons – and to watch the show.

That meant hard work for Elynne and Old Gidge, helping Aunt Pedda prepare food and drinks and other necessities.

Meanwhile Dan and Vennor went up on to the ridge to inspect the first group of dragons in the basin, and to make one last check on the sheds – where the people would gather, in safety, when it was time.

Hours later, as the sun was setting, Elynne was wearily piling even more small, freshly baked cakes on to a tray, while Aunt Pedda tirelessly mixed dough for another batch of biscuits. And then Gidge, who had gone to fetch water from the well, rushed back into the kitchen, eyes alight.

'There're *more!*' he cried. 'Just saw 'em, comin' down outa the clouds! *Hundreds* of 'em!'

Cakes and biscuits forgotten, Pedda and Elynne followed him out in a rush, finding Dan and Vennor in the yard. The sky was as overcast as before, but the new group of dragons had descended below the clouds, silhouetted against them. Not exactly hundreds, Elynne saw – but a splendid, terrifying horde, storming down towards the basin.

'Must be more than thirty, there,' Pedda said. 'Probably the last we'll get today.'

But it wasn't. As the horde settled, with the usual screeches and flapping of wings, they were suddenly silenced – when the sky seemed to be torn apart by the loudest, wildest dragon scream of all.

The sound made Elynne want to fall to the ground, or turn and run. But she stood rooted, petrified, as a huge shape erupted out of the clouds. Far bigger than any of the other dragons, with wings like giant sails, it swooped downwards in imperious circles.

And in that moment, a gap opened in the clouds, and a last ray of the sunset reached out like a spotlight to touch that enormous, solitary, late-coming dragon. The light flared on the scales of its armoured skin, which blazed as if they had been set on fire: A deep, rich, burnished red.

Chapter Three

A CRIMSON QUEEN

'Dragons aren't *red*,' Elynne whispered, astonished. But the others were all hurrying away towards the basin. Following uneasily, she caught up as they crept up the path into one of the viewing sheds, almost holding their breath to avoid disturbing the horde below them. And then they simply stared.

Dragons normally came in two sorts. The most numerous kind had dull grey scales – with the black wings and yellow eyes that *all* dragons had – and were about the size of a large dog. A smaller number, with dusty blue scales, were the size of a small pony. So the horde settling in the basin held mostly greys, with a dozen or so blues.

And one other.

'How can it be *red?*' Elynne asked softly.

Next to her, Old Gidge sighed. 'There're tales about a kind of extra-big dragon, livin' higher up than any other. A rare an' special breed, with red scales. Only a few, at any one time, so they got called the *royal* dragons. Never saw one before, myself, never.'

They all stared down at the red dragon, which was bigger than the biggest farm horse, bigger than any creature any of them had ever seen.

'See how the red's darker between the scales – deep crimson, nearly purple,' Pedda said. 'Probably born of ordinary blues. And it's a female.'

'A royal female,' Elynne said softly. 'A queen. A Crimson Queen.'

Dan Danneby grinned at her. 'That's *good*, Lynnie. We can use that. Because this time we *are* going to advertise. If we spread the word fast enough, we'll bring half the country here to see her.'

'If we could catch her an' keep her,' Vennor muttered, 'we could bring the *whole* country.'

As Dan silenced him with a look, Old Gidge shook his white head. 'No offence, Dan,' he said, 'but d'you think you can handle her?'

'Queen or not,' Dan said cheerily, 'she's a dragon. She can be charmed just like all the others.' He started towards the shed's door. 'Come on – we've work to do. People will start arriving tomorrow.'

They all trailed after him, except Elynne, who hung back for a moment. She noticed that the other dragons, the greys and blues, who normally jostled and snapped at each other as they settled in the basin, were keeping well clear of the giant red female. As if she really is their queen, Elynne thought. And the Crimson Queen was loftily ignoring the others, scooping a shallow pit for herself, like a nest, in the soft sand.

Elynne knew the horde would remain settled for the night and perhaps a day or two afterwards, never taking any food during their migratory flight. And the Queen, who had arrived later, might stay longer, since she would need more rest after the exertion of keeping her great body airborne. But still Elynne was reluctant to leave.

For that moment, safe in the shed, she didn't feel afraid. Instead, she felt a huge wonder and joy at seeing such a rarity as the Crimson Queen. And then, as if aware of her presence hidden in the shed, the great red dragon raised her head and stared directly up at Elynne, with a challenging yellow gaze.

Flinching, Elynne took an automatic step back from the viewing-slit. And she shivered as she wondered how anyone, even her fearless father, could dare even to think about going down into that basin.

She went to bed late, worn out from trying to keep up with her rushing, bustling aunt. Yet she woke early, with the shapeless edges of a dream melting in her mind.

Something terrible is going to happen, she thought.

She had no idea where the thought had come from, or what it meant. But it brought a coldness like the clutch of dead hands to her spine, pushing her out of bed in a hurry. Then she

looked out of the window and the feeling vanished.

The sun was up, the sky was cloudless, and the yard was swarming. People were everywhere, crowds of them, in carts and wagons, on horseback, wandering around on foot. And more were pouring in, and more, under the 'Dragon Charmer' sign. They were moving quietly, as people always did – all too aware of the menacing creatures only a meadow and a ridge away. And they were hurrying to rush their horses into the barn to safety, while the horses themselves trembled and rolled panicky eyes, with the scent of dragon in their nostrils.

The door slammed open and Elynne jumped. But it was only Aunt Pedda, as brisk and bustling as the night before.

'See the crowds?' Pedda said happily. 'There'll be more than one show today, I think. And we'll be rushed off our feet. Come along, love, if you want breakfast before we start.'

As it was, breakfast was a bit of bread gobbled on the run. Elynne and Pedda lugged heaped trays outside to trestle tables where Gidge cackled happily, raking in the coins as the swelling crowd bought and devoured the food.

Meanwhile Dan and Vennor were amassing more coins as they sold tickets, directing the people to gather beside the meadow.

'Thats all for now,' Dan said at last, when the milling group was enough to fill all the viewing sheds. But there were some left over, looking unhappy, and others still pouring in through the gate.

'We'll do another show later,' he promised, then grinned at Pedda. 'Keep them fed and happy,' he said. 'It'll be a long day.'

'We'll be *rich*!' Elynne breathed.

'No chance of that,' Vennor snarled.

But Elynne ignored him, as an older girl from Lowfield, the nearest village, came up with eager eyes. 'Is it true there's a *red* one?' she asked.

Elynne nodded proudly. 'A Crimson Queen.'

The other girl gasped excitedly, then ran to join her family as the crowd moved away along the path. And Elynne looked around at Aunt Pedda. 'Could I go and watch?' she begged.

Pedda laughed. 'Go on, then. I might watch the next show myself. You don't see *royalty* every day.'

Elynne raced away across the meadow, up the ridge's slope, into the nearest shed. Like the others it was crammed with people, all peering avidly down at the creatures in the natural arena of the basin. Especially at the huge, glistening-red shape of the Queen, nestled in the sand.

Such moments, at Dan Danneby's, were the

only times that most people would ever see a dragon, other than glimpsing a flying speck above distant mountain peaks. And so, despite the crowding in the sheds, everyone remained silent and motionless, gazing down with a mixture of tense excitement, curiosity and awe.

In that silence the Queen opened her eyes, and raised her majestic head.

At first it seemed to Elynne that the huge dragon was looking straight at *her* again. But the Queen was looking at something near the shed, on the ridge-top. And all of the people looked as well and gasped.

Dan Danneby was standing openly on the ridge, looking down at the dragons.

He had changed into his 'showman costume', as he called it – a white shirt with full sleeves, white trousers tucked into boots. Even Vennor, just behind him, had put on a clean shirt. They were both empty-handed, except for the strange object that each of them carried – like four slim cylinders of different lengths, fixed together side by side, with small holes along the length of them: a musical instrument called the dragon-pipes.

As the audience held its breath, Dan took a step forward. At once the Queen half-rose from the sand, spread her vast wings, and screamed. The frightful sound was deafening as it echoed up from the basin. And it was amplified by the voices of all the other dragons, flapping and screeching, readying their fangs and claws to deal with the intruders.

In the midst of that appalling din, Dan and Vennor raised the pipes to their mouths and began to play.

Slowly the music rose – hauntingly clear and pure, a delicate melody played by Dan swirling over a deeper, simpler line created by Vennor. Slowly, as the music floated out across the basin, the dragons' screeches faded, the flapping of their wings subsided.

And when all of them, including the Queen, had grown unbelievably still and silent, Dan and Vennor – still playing without pause – walked calmly down the inner slope of the basin.

Chapter Four

DRAGON TRANCE

As the two men reached the floor of the basin, the watching people heard another sound, deep and vibrant. It was like the distant song of bees, but there were no bees. It was a sleepy, humming sigh – coming from the throats of all the dragons, in harmony with the music that had silenced and entranced them.

As they hummed and the music floated around them, Vennor stopped at the edge of the basin while Dan stepped calmly forward.

With every note of his melody achingly pure, he walked into the midst of the dragons, close enough to touch them.

The watching people held their breath. They

all knew how murderously vicious even a small grey dragon could be – and the blues were worse. Yet Dan strolled among them, unconcerned, protected only by his music. And they all sat motionless, wings folded, eyes half-shut, humming their song.

Elynne had seen the dragon trance countless times, but she always responded the same way – with wonder and fear, and with a sadness that brought her to tears. It was wonderful to see how the unique music of the pipes always worked, on each and every dragon, without fail. Only a rare few became just slightly tranced, with the risk that they might suddenly awaken, in fury.

But the sadness that Elynne felt was entirely to do with herself. The show always brought back the memory of a time, years before, when everything had gone wrong for her – a time of failure and shame and screaming terror.

Though she had been very small at the time, she had learned some of the simpler passages of the dragon-charming music. But while many people might learn to play the pipes, the greatest

musicians in the world could not hope to charm dragons if they lacked the special, mysterious, inner power. So, back then, Dan had decided it was time to see if Elynne had inherited the power to go with the music. And he had taken her with her pipes to the basin, where a handful of dragons had landed in the spring migration.

At first, when she had played the simple melody, it had begun to work. The dragons had seemed to start slipping into the humming trance. So, pleased and excited, she had started to move towards the dragons before Dan could stop her. But her small feet had stumbled, her fingers had slipped, the music had faltered, and the moment had been lost.

Instantly, as the melody halted, the dragons had launched themselves with a monstrous shrieking towards her.

Dan had scooped her up and sprinted for a shed, slamming the door and the view-slit shutter just in time. For moments that had seemed like years, the dragons raged outside, hurling themselves at the shed walls, clawing at its thatched roof — while Elynne screamed in mindless panic inside. And though Dan's dragon-pipes had eventually calmed and tranced the dragons, the damage had been done.

Elynne's terror had never subsided. She had had nightmares for months, and she had avoid-ed the dragon – charming show for many seasons. Above all, she had somehow become unable to play the pipes. Whenever she tried, remembered terror made her fingers too tense and anxious to produce anything beyond off-key discords.

Aunt Pedda said that her playing, and her dragon – charming power too, was being choked and blocked by her fear of dragons. But know-ing that was no help.

She would have sacrificed anything to be able to walk out into that basin with her father. Or even to be like Vennor, whose weaker power forced him to stay back from the horde. Aunt Pedda always said that Vennor's dragon-charm-ing gift was stunted by his sour, sullen nature – but at least he can use it, Elynne thought.

[39]

I wish I were different, she thought mournfully. I wish I weren't me.

Remembering it all once again, she had more or less stopped watching what was going on in the basin, where the white-clad figure of her father was still moving among the motionless dragons, still playing the hypnotic music. But when all the people around her gasped, she came back to the present with a jolt.

A big blue dragon – clearly less affected by the trancing – had opened its eyes and half-flared its wings as Dan went by.

Neither Dan nor the music faltered. Calmly he strengthened the melody and the power that it carried. And the blue dragon subsided back into the peaceful trance.

And *that's* why Niys Vennor stays back, Elynne reminded herself. Because he hasn't got enough of the power to do that. The blue dragon would have torn *him* to shreds.

So, she thought with a shudder, what would they do to *me?*

Quickly she forced the thought away – because

the show's finale was starting.

Having strolled around and past every one of the dragons, including the Crimson Queen, Dan came to a halt in their midst, subtly altering the music. As the new melody swelled out, still haunting and eerie but with a different tempo, the dragons began to stir.

Again the people gasped – but the creatures weren't waking. They were moving in their trance – as dragons always did when stirred in that way by the dragon-pipes.

Slowly their wings lifted, their necks stretched out. Slowly their heads began to sway, back and forth, in time with the music, in eerie, perfect unison. Then their bodies began to move, swaying from side to side, with small shuffling steps to keep their balance. Always together, always in step, in a magical unity as if they had been practising for months.

And Dan moved quietly among them, playing – now and then actually *touching* one of them, gently helping it to move slightly to give itself more room.

Until at last the formation was perfect, near-ly half a hundred dragons in more or less straight lines, wings half-raised and eyes half-shut, swaying and stepping exactly together, rapt in the enchantment of the music.

With, as a special extra amazement, the Crim-son Queen at the centre of the formation, huge and gleaming and glorious.

Still playing the new melody, Dan began carefully to move back out of their midst. Still entranced around him, the dragons swayed and stepped. And then, from the edge of the basin, for no apparent reason, Niys Vennor played a grating, discordant phrase.

It was only an instant's lapse and hardly any of the dragons seemed to be affected, not even the big blue that had half-awakened before. But Dan was still in the midst of the horde, only a stride from the Crimson Queen.

And with the harshness of Vennor's mistake, the Queen opened her huge yellow eyes, bared fearsome fangs, and struck at Dan with blurring speed.

Chapter Five

AMAZING ARRIVAL

Luckily, Dan had been looking towards the Queen, and experience warned him when her eyes first began to open. He flung himself back in a flailing leap, almost colliding with a grey as the Queen's great teeth clashed only a hand's breadth away.

Before she could continue the attack, Dan found his feet with miraculous agility and coolness, and began to play again. The melody rose, soothing and sweet, while Vennor – looking guilt-stricken – played on with desperate concentration.

Recaptured by the trance, the Queen's eyes closed and she sank back into the quiet humming and swaying.

[43]

The audience had been frozen in silent horror, and were all gasping and sighing with huge relief as Dan climbed back out of the basin with Vennor, continuing the music until they were over the ridge. And Elynne, struggling not to cry with her own relief, found she had bitten her lip hard enough to make it bleed.

But she ignored the hurt as she rushed out of the shed with all the other people gathering around Dan with excited cries, full of praise and admiration. And Dan smiled politely, and thanked them, and winked at Elynne.

'The dragons will stay tranced for a while,' he said in reply to a question. 'But they'll all be fine when they come round. No after-effects.'

'Do they often wake up suddenly like that?' a woman asked shakily. 'I mean, it must be so *dangerous*.'

'They hardly ever come completely out of the trance like that,' Dan told her with a shrug. 'I suppose accidents happen – I was lucky.'

Everyone turned to look at Vennor, who stared sullenly down at his boots and said nothing. If only I could do it, Elynne thought woefully, as she did so often. I'd make sure there were no accidents. I *wish* I could be brave.

'Where did the big red one come from, Dan?' asked a man from Lowfield. 'It's a beauty!'

'No idea,' Dan said easily. 'They say the royal dragons usually find their own private, secret places to rest when they migrate.' He grinned. 'You'll have to ask her what she's doing here.'

Everyone laughed and began to troop away

back to the farmyard, perhaps for more of Pedda's cooking before setting off home. Some of them wanted to buy new tickets to see it all over again – and Elynne could see an enormous crowd down in the yard, waiting impatiently for their turn.

This is more than we used to get in a *week*, she thought dazedly. All because of the Queen.

And so it proved. Dan did two more shows that day, which went off without any more frights. But then, though there were still more people waiting, he stopped, announcing that he and Vennor were getting tired. And it wasn't a good idea to be tired, and perhaps careless, around a dragon horde.

Most of the people went away uncomplainingly, many of them promising to be back. And so, after that amazing day – when their earnings from ticket and food sales amounted to a 'small fortune', as Gidge said – the following days were just as exciting and successful. Because the star attraction seemed in no hurry to leave.

As usual, some of the blues and greys flew

away on the second day to continue their migration – but others flew in to make up the numbers. The same thing happened on the third day, and the fourth. But during all those days, the Crimson Queen stayed where she was, nestling in her hollow of soft sand, except for visits to the pool for a drink.

'It's worrying,' Dan said at last, on the evening of the fourth day, when they were all relaxing wearily in the house. 'She's hardly moved all day. She doesn't even move much in the trance.'

'At least she hasn't jumped you again,' Old Gidge said with a grin.

'I don't think she would, now,' Dan said. 'There's something wrong.'

Pedda nodded. 'Royal or not, she isn't behaving the way dragons do.'

'You mean she's *sick*?' Elynne cried, distressed.

'She could be,' Dan said sadly.

Vennor sniffed. 'If she dies here, we could have her stuffed – charge extra to see her.'

'She's *not* going to die!' Elynne flared. 'We can't *let* her!'

Dan patted her shoulder. 'I hope she won't, honey – but there's nothing we can do to help her.'

The worry increased next day, when more dragons left and none arrived to take their place, and the migration came to its normal end. Yet still the Queen sat dozing in her sandy nest, looking as if she were never going anywhere, heavy and sluggish during the dragon-charming show.

On the sixth day, she was alone in the basin. And when a few people turned up asking for even a one-dragon show, Dan politely turned them away. 'We think she's unwell,' he told them. 'We'll let her be.'

So those incredible autumn shows – 'we took more money than we usually get in four autumns and four springs,' Aunt Pedda said – came to an end. But for Elynne especially, delight at their success was over-shadowed by the condition of the Queen. Elynne spent most of the seventh day up in a viewing shed, watching as the Queen sat like a motionless crimson statue, with only the movement of her sides to show that she was still breathing.

But in the middle of that night, the Crimson Queen came shockingly to life.

It was an overcast and thundery night, with tongues of lightning licking among the clouds. The air was too heavy and humid for anyone to sleep well. And then, in the darkest heart of the night, sleep became impossible.

A scream arose from the basin – a piercing, nerve-scraping dragon screech, ripping through the night and the silence, clutching at Elynne with the icy claws of fear. It was a shriek that seemed to arise out of some unknown agony, yet tinged somehow with a weird note of *triumph*.

They all dashed out in their night-clothes, Dan and Gidge with lanterns. Rushing up to the ridge, they ducked into one of the sheds and stared down at the basin.

The lantern-light reached far enough to show that the Queen was still there in the sandy hollow, alive and awake. But she looked as if she had gone mad, berserk. She was half-lifted up on her powerful hind legs, wings widespread, eyes glittering and fangs glinting in the light. And as she saw the light at the top of the ridge, those fangs parted more widely with another spine-freezing shriek, full of fury and menace.

In the same instant, as if summoned by her scream, the sky above was filled with the spearing, dazzling glory of lightning. And in its brightness they all glimpsed what lay at the great dragon's feet, the cause of her frenzy.

An object larger than a human head, smoothly gleaming as if newly polished, brilliantly rose-pink.

A royal dragon egg.

Chapter Six

HOPES AND THREATS

The Queen soon settled back again, covering the egg, as if deciding that the light in the shed was no more dangerous to her than the lightning in the sky. And the five people moved slowly away, stunned by the miracle they had seen.

Almost no one ever got to see a dragon's egg. Dragons made their nests on the highest, most inaccessible crags. Few people dared to climb so high — and if any had been brave or mad enough to try to reach a dragon's nest, they had not survived the attempt.

But there was an egg in the basin. A new-laid, living egg — and a *royal* egg. A Crimson Prince or Princess, Elynne thought, marvelling.

Then in her daze she became aware that Vennor was speaking to her father, in an insistent and angry mutter.

'It's worth more'n you could *count* in a year!' Vennor was snarling. 'It's the chance of a lifetime! You can't just let it go! We got some say in all this, too . . .'

'We have,' Aunt Pedda broke in. 'And I say that Dan's right. For all we know, these might be the last two royal dragons anywhere!'

'Right,' Gidge agreed. 'Whatever Dan says is fine with me.'

Vennor's hands clenched into fists. 'How can you be so *stupid?* There are rich folk around who'd pay what this whole *valley's* worth to get that egg!'

'But they aren't going to get it,' Dan said flatly. 'Niys, I've told you. I'm not in the business of caging wild dragons — and I'm *definitely* not in the business of stealing a royal egg.'

As Vennor began again to protest, Dan held up a hand, his eyes steely. 'No — I don't want to hear any more. We're leaving the Queen alone, and that's that.'

He stalked away, and the others followed – though Vennor glanced hungrily around once more at the basin, where the Queen crouched protectively over her precious egg.

But in the morning, when curiosity and concern drew them all back to look again, the basin was deserted.

Their distress lasted only briefly – for as their voices rose in shock, they heard a menacing growl from the next shed along. And when they warily peered through that shed's viewing-slit, they saw the Crimson Queen – with her egg intact – resting on a huge crude nest made from torn-up grass and brush. Then they dodged back, as the Queen glared and snarled at them.

'She must've been working since first light!' Pedda gasped, as they moved away.

Gidge laughed shakily. 'Someone musta left the shed door open. She's made herself at home.'

Dan nodded. 'It can't be too easy for her to carry the egg, let alone fly any distance with it.

So she's decided to stay.'

Vennor grunted. 'I hope you're gonna spread the word. Folk will pay to see that.'

'No,' Dan said firmly. 'She's to be left in peace. Though we might do something when the egg hatches.'

'If it hatches,' Vennor muttered. 'If it don't break or go rotten or somethin'.'

'It'd be interesting,' Dan went on, ignoring him, 'to try the pipes on a dragon hatchling.'

With that, Elynne became lost in a dream – of finally finding the dragon – charming ability within herself, and practising on the new-hatched dragon that had become tame, her pet and her friend.

So, in the time that followed – while the Crimson Queen stayed safe in the shed, being taken food from Pedda's kitchen – Elynne struggled harder than ever before to master the dragon-pipes. Without any success at all.

Until, at last, three days later, her frustration and misery grew so great that she hurled the pipes across her room and flung herself on her bed in a tempest of tearful fury that brought her father worriedly to her door.

'I'll *never* do it!' she cried. 'Never! It's *hopeless!*'

Dan shook his head sympathetically. 'That may be true, Lynnie. But it's not the end of the world. There are other things to do.'

'I don't *want* other things!' she yelled furiously. 'It's not *fair!* Why can't I be a dragon charmer too?'

'You know why,' Dan said gently, putting an

arm around her. 'You were so badly frightened, that time. The fear is like a *disease*, getting in your way – even when you just try to play the pipes.'

She pressed her tearful face against his shoulder. 'Then it is hopeless! How can I stop being *afraid*?'

'It can be done.' Dan said. 'A person *can* get over fear – mostly by wanting something. Wanting to have or to do or to *be* something – wanting so badly, so fiercely, that they stop caring about all the things that make them afraid. If you wanted something that much, Lynnie, you wouldn't let *anything* get in your way – not even your fear.'

Her sigh was almost a sob. 'But I *do* want to be a dragon charmer.'

'Then keep trying.' Dan said, smiling. 'And don't give up hope.'

Later that day Elynne was gloomily thinking about her father's words, still feeling miserable and useless and despairing. Her father had gone with Aunt Pedda into Lowfield village for some supplies, but Elynne had stayed behind, moping around the house and finally out into the yard.

From the paddock Donnie the donkey looked at her hopefully, as always, but she wandered past, heading for the ridge as if drawn by a magnet, for another wistful look at the Queen. Trailing up the path, she was moving carefully through the brush, to avoid disturbing the dragon, when she was startled by the sound of men's voices – and chilled by what they were saying.

'You really sure you can keep the big one quiet, an' out of the way?' one voice was saying – a hard, rough voice that Elynne had never heard before.

But the reply came in a voice she knew.

'Don't you worry', said the snarling voice of Niys Vennor. 'There's lots of ways to keep it quiet. If we have to, we can kill it.'

Chapter Seven

FEARFUL CRIME

Holding her breath, Elynne crept forward through the brush. A few leaves rustled as she moved, a twig or two crackled – but the men's voices covered those sounds.

'Ain't no need to hurry,' the man with the rough voice was saying. 'Wait for the right night, when there's no moon – maybe with rain, to cover any noise we make. Anyways, I'm waitin' for the other two to get here. We could need 'em if we run into trouble.'

'That's not likely,' Vennor replied. 'Nobody'll be anywhere near.'

Peering through a cluster of leaves, heart thumping, Elynne saw the two men on the inner

slope of the ridge, down near the basin, alarm-
ingly close to where she crouched. The man with
Vennor looked truly dangerous – big and bulky,
with a grim, heavy-browed face. But still both
men seemed certain that they were alone and
unheard.

'When it's done,' the bulky stranger was saying,
'we'll stay in my place, over in Fallwood, while
we put the word out to some likely buyers.'

'An' then go get rich,' Vennor said with
an evil chuckle. 'Right, Strack. Send word when
you're ready.'

The two then parted, Vennor moving up the slope towards the path, the other man, Strack, heading towards the road to Lowfield. Elynne shrank back into the brush as Vennor passed, then crept out after a few breathless moments and hurried home without looking at the Queen, deeply troubled.

Vennor was clearly planning some kind of crime, with Strack and two other men – for what else would need silence and secrecy on a rainy, moonless night? Maybe a robbery, she thought. That'd be just like Niys Vennor, always so greedy for money. And they were planning to hide out in Fallwood, wherever that was, with their booty.

She halted, shivering as if she had been embedded in a block of ice. It suddenly occurred to her what the 'booty' might be.

The Crimson Queen's precious egg, of course. Vennor had said it was worth as much as the whole of the Woodfern Valley.

Still, she couldn't be sure. Her first instinct was to tell her father, but she couldn't see exactly what there was to tell. She might be on the wrong track altogether, just because she didn't like Vennor. He and Strack hadn't really said anything about stealing, in so many words. Vennor might have a perfectly innocent explanation, which would make her look foolish, and would make him even nastier towards her, if she started accusing him.

Hesitant and anxious, she decided to say nothing about it just yet, but to keep an eye on Vennor, hoping to learn more about what he was up to, perhaps finding the proof she needed, before the next rainy night came along.

But, over the next few days, Vennor did nothing unusual, no matter how closely she watched him. Nor was there any further sign of Strack. Nor was there any change in the egg, which could sometimes be glimpsed – rosy-pink, gleaming, motionless – in the Queen's nest.

So, even though the weather remained fine and clear, day and night, Elynne's tension and anxiety steadily mounted until she was almost wild with nervous desperation. She knew she was running out of time, and yet she still had nothing to prove any accusation that she might bring against Vennor. Night after night, as time went on, she peered up at the sky, praying that no rain-clouds would drift in to aid the robbers, wishing that she didn't have to sleep so that she could be constantly on guard.

As it was, with all that tension, she was sleeping badly and waking early. As she did on one particular morning, upon hearing a disturbing sound, and smelling a troubling smell.

The rosy glow at her window told her that it was just before sunrise, yet the sound she could hear was the voice of Old Gidge, not renowned as an early riser. Gidge and Vennor had adjoining rooms in a lean-to addition at the back of the house – and Gidge had come to rouse Dan with some troubling news.

'... never came in last night, never slept in his bed,' Gidge was saying worriedly. 'An' there's no sign of him anywhere.'

Elynne's eyes opened wide – just as she recognised the troubling smell. The fresh, clean smell of wet grass and damp earth. After a *rainfall* . . .

An instant later, she flashed past the two startled men in the doorway. Running like a frightened deer across the rain-soaked meadow and up the ridge, she leaped to the viewing-slit of the Crimson Queen's shed, and peered in.

At first the early morning dimness in the shed defeated her vision, yet still her heart seemed to leap and flutter as if trying to escape. The shed was silent. No growling, no shifting of great claws or flaring of wings.

And then her eyes adjusted enough to let her see – and she screamed.

The Queen lay beside her nest, on her back, eyes shut. The movement of her scaly sides showed that she was breathing, so she was merely asleep. But also, unbelievably, her powerful limbs and wings were bound by heavy ropes.

Yet that was not what had made Elynne scream.

It was the fact that the nest itself, the heap of grass and brush where the dragon egg should have gleamed as rosily as the dawn, lay empty.

Chapter Eight

DRAGON FURY

Elynne whirled away from the dreadful sight, almost hysterical with horror, and nearly crashed into Dan – coming worriedly after her with Gidge, even more quickly after they heard her scream.

Dan hugged her tightly, asking what was wrong. But as she gasped and sobbed, trying to find the words, Gidge glanced into the shed – and there was no more need for explanations.

'How could anyone tie up a *dragon?*' the old man asked shakily. Then he stiffened as he realised. 'Less they tranced her, first.'

'It was Niys Vennor!' Elynne shrieked, finding her voice. 'I know it was. I heard him and the other man! And I could have *stopped* them!'

She began another storm of weeping. But as Dan held her and soothed her, and as Aunt Pedda came to find out what all the fuss was, she finally grew calm enough to tell her story 'And if I'd only *said* something,' she said at the end, her voice breaking with despair, 'I could have stopped them. . .'

Dan shook his head, keeping an arm around her. 'Don't blame yourself, Lynnie. It was natural to hold back, if you weren't really sure.'

'Only one person to blame,' Aunt Pedda snapped. 'If I could get my hands on that Vennor . . .'

'I'd like that myself,' Dan said grimly. 'But first we have to help the Queen.'

'Careful, now,' Gidge warned.

'It'll be all right,' Dan replied. 'Vennor must have tranced her, as you said.'

'Vennor ain't as good at it as you are,' Gidge reminded him.

Dan stepped towards the shed door. 'She still seems far enough under. And I don't want to leave her roped up for another second.'

Fighting back the last of her tears, Elynne watched him move into the shed, towards the motionless dragon. With a sturdy pocket-knife, he began sawing at one of the heavy ropes.

And with shocking suddenness, the Crimson Queen awoke.

As her eyes opened, she began fighting her bonds with all her immense power. The rope that Dan had half-cut broke with an explosive *crack*, some hastily tied knots tore or pulled apart – and the mighty dragon surged to her feet, clawing the ropes away.

Instantly Dan leaped for the door. But as the Queen freed herself, she flung her vast wings wide. One wing struck Dan with the force of a battering ram, and hurled him with a splinter-ing crash against the wall of the shed.

As he crumpled in an unconscious heap, Elynne screamed again. But no one heard her – for the Queen, ignoring Dan, whirled with a screech of her own to claw at the dry brush of her nest.

And when she found that the egg was gone, she screamed a last anguished scream, and hurtled straight up. Wings thrashing, she blasted through the roof's wooden rafters and thick thatching as if they were as thin as thistledown – arrowing away like a bolt of crimson fire into a sky itself ablaze with sunrise.

At once Pedda and Gidge dashed into the shed, with Elynne stumbling after them as Gidge cautiously turned Dan over to reveal a dripping gash on his forehead and an oddly bent arm.

'That arm's broken,' Pedda muttered tensely. 'Maybe some ribs too. But his head looks worst of all.'

'Is he going to die?' Elynne gasped, her voice shaking.

Pedda turned, gripping her by the shoulders. 'No, of course not,' she snapped. 'But you're going to have to stop crying and find some *grit*, Elynne, because you're *needed*.' Her gaze was fierce, demanding. 'I'm going to try and stop the bleeding while Gidge gets a barrow to carry Dan back to the house. Which means *you're* going to have to go for the doctor.'

'The doctor?' Elynne whimpered. 'Me?'

'Doctor Ward, in the village,' her aunt said. 'Ride the donkey in, and bring the doctor back as fast as you can.' Her grip tightened. 'There's no one else, love. You *have* to do it – for your father!'

The appeal jolted Elynne into action. Rushing away with Gidge, fighting hard against a desire to collapse in a heap and cry her heart out, she got herself dressed, fumbled a bridle over Donnie's head and rode away on the road to Lowfield. The little donkey seemed to understand the urgency, trotting along with sure-footed speed while Elynne sat limply, seeing not the road but the ghastly images of that morning all over again – the empty nest, the Queen's fury, her father's dire injuries.

At last they reached the village, still half-asleep in the early morning. She had never been to Lowfield by herself before, and she had had very little to do with Doctor Ward – yet somehow in the turmoil of that morning she felt none of her usual shyness and timidity. Instead, she was moving in a sort of numbed calm, as she quickly managed to find Doctor Ward and tell him about Dan. In no time they were setting off in his one-horse carriage, with the donkey tied behind.

Doctor Ward, a kindly man, listened with amazement and made comforting replies as Elynne also told him, numbly, about the theft of the dragon's egg and the flight of the Crimson Queen. But there was little comfort to be found back at the farmstead, where Dan was still unconscious, though Pedda had stopped the bleeding from his head-wound.

'His arm is badly broken,' the doctor said at last, 'and so are two ribs – and I'm fairly sure that his skull is fractured as well. But he's strong and healthy. If he stays in bed, and stays as quiet as possible, he should mend, in time, without too much trouble.'

'He won't like that,' Aunt Pedda sighed. 'I know Dan. He'll want to be up and after those thieves, to get the egg back.'

Doctor Ward snorted. 'He'll do no such thing – not with a skull fracture. If he doesn't stay as quiet as possible, he could do himself grave harm.'

As Elynne stared worriedly at her motionless father, the doctor took some twists of paper from his medical bag. 'Use these sleeping powders if he needs them,' he went on. 'And when he wakes up, make him understand that he must stay quiet, while he mends. There can be no rushing around after dragon eggs or anything else for him.'

Chapter Nine

DESPERATE PLAN

Fresh misery flooded through Elynne at the doctor's words – a misery rising partly from worry about her father, but even more from guilt and shame. It's all my fault, she thought wretchedly. I should have told them about Vennor. And now everything is ruined, and no one can do anything – and I'm to blame . . .

'Of course,' Doctor Ward was saying to Aunt Pedda, 'you could report all this to Constable Brine.'

Pedda sniffed dismissively. Constable Brine, Lowfield's village policeman, fat and slow and getting old, was unlikely to gallop in pursuit of a gang of robbers. And anyway, the doctor pointed out, it wasn't as if the egg actually *belonged* to anyone . . .

'It's too bad though, it really is,' the doctor went on sympathetically. 'Never liked that Vennor myself. And he's been keeping rough company lately, in Lowfield – a big ugly fellow named something like Strack, from over in Greenbriar Valley, and two other strangers who arrived a few days ago.'

In the midst of her misery Elynne lifted her head. Greenbriar was the name of the next valley, to the east of their own Woodfern. She had never been there, but she knew how to reach it – along the main road eastwards, then through the craggy Raketooth Hills by means of the Slipstone Gap.

'In Greenbriar Valley,' she asked carefully, 'is there a place called Fallwood?'

Doctor Ward nodded. 'There's a village of that name. Why?'

'Just wondering,' Elynne said vaguely.

But she was remembering what she had overheard Strack telling Vennor. That they would lie low, after the robbery, at his place – in Fallwood. So that was where the Queen's egg probably was, right then.

Still, she wondered unhappily, what good did it do to know that? Aunt Pedda and Old Gidge weren't likely to go after Vennor and the egg. Nor was the useless Constable Brine, nor anyone else – since everyone would probably agree with the doctor that the egg hadn't really been *stolen* from anyone. But it *has*, she thought. It's ours more than anyone's. But above all, it belongs to the Crimson Queen.

'I would have liked to have seen that egg,' the doctor said regretfully. 'A lot of people would have paid good money to see it.'

'That's so.' Pedda agreed glumly. 'Though of course Dan will be more upset over losing the egg itself than the money. He'll be near as sick about it as the Queen herself. He does love the dragons.'

The words silenced Elynne completely, plunging her even deeper into shame and self-blame, all tangled up with anxiety about her father and a bitter, helpless rage towards Niys Vennor. For her, in that storm of misery, the hours that followed were empty and meaningless, when she did nothing but relive, over and over, the terrible events of the morning. Her mind reeled under the endless assault of guilt and sorrow and despair threatening to overwhelm her, to damage her beyond repair.

And so, in nature's way of things, her mind began to protect itself. To keep the emotional storms at bay, it put up a *shield* – an inner wall.

Behind the protection of that mental wall Elynne again grew calm, in a blank, numbed way. She was even able to think about what had happened without being battered and crushed by misery. And also, behind the protection of the inner wall, something else began to take shape. Something quite new, and odd, and unfamiliar.

That became clear in a crucial moment when she found herself facing the four basic, undeniable, unbearable *facts* of that day's disaster. First, her father was out of action, dangerously injured. Second, by the time he was better it would be too late for him to search for the egg. Third, that loss was mostly her fault, for being too timid to speak up. Fourth, no one could do anything to fix things.

At least . . . no one *else* could.

When those last four words entered her mind, as if by themselves, they stopped her in her tracks. She was vaguely aware that once she would have cowered away in tremulous dread from those words. But from behind her protective inner wall, she could consider them coolly and dispassionately.

No one could do anything to fix things – except *her*.

Distantly, within her inner blankness, she felt a surge that was like a desperate hunger. Right then, she had never wanted anything more in her life than to thwart the hated Vennor and rescue the egg. And, she thought, she *should* be the one to do it – not just because she had let the disaster happen, but because she alone knew where the egg *was*.

And as that hunger grew in her mind, fed by anger and yearning and desperation, something else began to grow from it. Some frail, vulnerable seeds of resolve, of *determination*, began to take root.

Behind her protective wall she was aware of raw foaming terror trying to break through, to sweep over her. But the wall resisted, so the terror could be ignored. And the vague, wishful idea grew into an intention, and hardened into a plan.

Without any more hesitation, before doubt could let the terror through, she went quickly to collect a small packet of food, extra clothes, and an old blanket to wrap them in. Pedda and Gidge were busy elsewhere, wrapped in their own worries, paying little attention to her. So they didn't see her creep into her father's room, to see if he was all right despite his ugly wounds. And the sight of him added new fuel to her rage at Vennor, and fed those tiny seeds within her of growing determination.

On impulse, vaguely thinking that she might

need it, she pocketed one of the twists of paper that held Dan's sleeping powders, before leaving the room. Outside, still unnoticed, she put the bridle on Donnie the donkey, then climbed on to his back with her bundle.

And no one saw them as they rode away.

Chapter Ten

FALLWOOD

Before long the curve of the road left the farmstead out of sight behind her. In her sudden sense of aloneness, a new wave of terror hurled itself against her internal wall. The wall wavered – and the terror swelled.

Around her, the familiar landscape appeared suddenly strange and menacing. In the fields, unnerving shadows among the bushes writhed like living things in the breeze, unseen birds and insects made noises like distant crazed voices. Far ahead, the Raketooth Hills rose in their rocky tiers like an immense fanged mouth, waiting to engulf her.

While before much longer, night would

descend on the land – leaving her alone and unprotected in darkness.

So her terror expanded, in thunderous new onslaughts. And her inner wall wavered again, and began to crumble.

She drew Donnie to a halt and sat there, trembling. 'I can't *do* this,' she said aloud, her voice quavering.

The donkey's ears twitched, and he half-turned his head to gaze at her with a gentle brown eye.

'Donnie . . . I can't, really,' she quavered. 'It's impossible. I'm so frightened . . .'

The donkey snorted softly.

'I know,' Elynne said, as if Donnie had replied. 'I shouldn't give up. Not when everything has gone so wrong. But *anything* could happen out here. I don't know what made me think I could do it . . . I've never done anything brave. I've never even *been* anywhere much, all by myself.'

The donkey snorted again, lightly stamping a forefoot.

'All right,' she said, again as if he had spoken. 'I suppose I'm not all by myself. You're here. But what can we *do*? Except get into trouble, and make everything worse.'

Donnie shook his head – to get rid of a fly, but it looked like disagreement. And Elynne fell silent, feeling oddly abashed, as if she had been rebuked.

'I know,' she said at last, unhappily. 'I'm being a weepy coward again . . . I wish I weren't – but I can't help it.'

Donnie stood silent and motionless, still looking round at her, as if waiting. And in that moment of poised stillness she saw again the images of her father – the Queen's empty nest – Vennor's sneering face. And the seeds of determination that had rooted within her stirred again.

She took a deep, shuddering breath, took a firmer grip on the reins. 'Maybe I should start trying to help it,' she murmured. 'Maybe . . .'

The donkey tossed his head up and down, as if nodding. And shakily, faintly, but definitely, Elynne managed to nod as well.

'All right,' she said, patting Donnie. 'We'll go on for a while, and look after each other, and I'll try not to be cowardly. Maybe something good will happen.'

The donkey seemed to nod again, and picked up his pace as if eager to get on with things. So, in a short while, they arrived again within sight of Lowfield.

For a moment Elynne thought about seeing if someone there would put her up for the night. But she couldn't face the thought of explaining herself to semi-strangers and having them try to make her go home rather than continue with her quest. And while the fearful part of her badly *wanted* to go home, the other part held grimly on to its new-found determination. She had no wish, she thought stubbornly, to be *made* to go home.

So she turned Donnie off the road – skirting around Lowfield through fields and brush, un-seen, before returning to the road on the far side of the village.

There, as Donnie trotted on eastwards, terror returned. The land east of Lowfield was far less familiar to her, and was weirdly, ominously silent, as if holding its breath, waiting for some dreadful happening. And before much longer the road began to slope slightly upwards, reminding her of steeper slopes to come, when they would cross over the Slipstone Gap and down into the Greenbriar Valley, to the unknown village of Fallwood. Where the enemy was.

Worst of all, as the road began its upward slope, the shadows of evening were creeping in all around her.

Once again, dread and panic rose ravening within her. And she no longer had a protective wall of blank numbness to hold them off. She was shivering, though the evening remained warm. She flinched at every rustling leaf, saw monsters in every shadow. Part of her urgently wanted to turn and run for home and safety.

Yet she didn't. Despite everything, her newly rooted determination held out. Even more astonishingly to her, it gave her the will to fight back, desperately, heroically, against the fear.

And, for nearly the first time in her life, she was *winning*.

She was still armed with her anger and resolve and a burning wish to make things better. She also had Donnie's warm, solid presence and the knowledge that they had travelled some distance for most of a day without seeing anything more menacing than a fly. As a defence it wasn't much, but it helped to reassure her.

And she was also helped by remembering what her father had told her, not long before. She could almost hear him, as if he were there with her, in the darkness.

'A person can get over fear,' Dan had told her, 'by *wanting* something so badly that they stop caring about all the things that make them afraid.'

And I do so badly want to get the egg back, she thought fiercely, and make everything all right again.

So she battled against the swarming terrors — and slowly, laboriously, drove them back. Not far, perhaps, but far enough to let her get on with what she had to do.

In the last glimmering of twilight, she decided

to leave the road and look for a safe place for the night. She turned Donnie into some fields with patches of trees and bushes, and there good fortune brought her to a perfect spot – a secluded thicket with soft turf underfoot and even a brook gurgling nearby.

There she tried to settle. Donnie happily drank from the brook and grazed on the turf, while Elynne nibbled without appetite at the food she had brought. Before long, weary after travelling, Donnie went peacefully to sleep. And because of his peace, and the brook's soothing sound, and her own weariness, Elynne was able to push her fears back even further. Wrapped in her blanket, she fell asleep as well.

When she woke, with a start, she found that the sun was up, Donnie was contentedly breakfasting on the turf, and everything was entirely, astoundingly peaceful. She had spent a night in the open, in a strange place, all by herself – and nothing at all had happened to her.

The small fearful part of her mind tried to say that something still could happen, if she kept going. But the newly determined part of her ignored that thought. It pointed out that she had been afraid of being alone, and being outside by herself all night, yet no dangers had appeared. So maybe other things, which seemed terrifying when she *thought* about them, might not be so terrible when they actually happened.

Unhesitatingly, she gathered her things, mounted Donnie, and rode away.

Nonetheless, her fears returned again during the morning. The road steadily became steeper and rougher, winding upwards between harsh slopes and bleak ridges. Soon it also grew narrower, with looming walls of rock on either side. Yet still Elynne clung to her determination, keeping her mind fixed as firmly as she could on her purpose.

Finally, on the crest of the Slipstone Gap, she halted for a rest and a midday snack, with the spikes and ridges and cliffs of the Raketooth Hills rising around her. Then, through the early afternoon, she and Donnie continued steadily on – down the far slope of the Gap, into the open lushness of the Greenbriar Valley. And finally, after more time, into the village of Fallwood.

It looked very like the village of Lowfield, with a few shops, a blacksmith, a tavern and so on along the road, and clusters of houses on either side. Entering it, she was gripped by new fright at the thought that Vennor might be near and would see her. But there were only a few people visible, all strangers, and her anxiety eased.

Gathering her nerve, she asked a woman if she knew where a man named Strack lived. But she couldn't help flinching when the woman glared.

'Strack?' the woman snapped. 'What d'you want with the likes of *him*?'

Elynne thought quickly. 'My . . . er . . . uncle is visiting him.'

The woman sniffed. 'If you must find him, he lives beyond the village, there.' She pointed. 'Follow the path that you'll see through the woods.'

Elynne thanked her and began to turn away, but the woman reached out as if to stop her. 'It may be no business of mine, child,' she said, 'but I must warn you. Everyone here knows Strack to be a rough and violent man. Around him, uncle or no, you could be in danger.'

Chapter Eleven

ROBBERS ROBBED

The woman had pointed Elynne towards a slope of land at the far end of the village, covered with trees and undergrowth. She found the path at once, but hesitated, peering nervously into the shadowy woods.

Somewhere in there, at the end of the sloping path, the enemy lurked. Four dangerous robbers – Vennor, Strack and their two helpers – guarding the dragon's egg. The thought made her shiver, as once again the fearfulness gathered. What did she think she could *do*, she asked herself, if she found them? March in and demand that they give the egg back?

But then Donnie twitched his head, as if to

urge her on, and she tightened her jaw and clenched her fists. There's no danger *here*, right *now*, she told herself firmly. Just go up the path a way, and take a look.

She led Donnie into the woods, moving with small nervous steps, peering all around, tensing with every flicker of a leaf. But she went on.

Until she heard the voices.

They were rough, deep, men's voices, one of them sounding like Strack. And they seemed to be around the next bend of the path, only a few steps ahead.

In a near-panic, Elynne dodged aside into the woods, pulling the surprised donkey after her. As the greenery closed around them she was almost sobbing with fright, certain that her gasps and Donnie's hooves would have been heard by the men. Halting, her arms around Donnie's neck, she peered back towards the path.

But the men were still talking, hearing nothing beyond their own voices and heavy footsteps. Through the leaves Elynne caught glimpses of them, and saw that there were only three - the bulky Strack and two others almost as big. With no sign of Niys Vennor.

'You sure this'll be all right?' one of the other two men was asking. 'Goin' into the village like this, out in the open?'

'Course,' Strack growled. 'I told you – all we've done is take a wild dragon's egg. It didn't belong to Danneby or anybody else, so takin' it isn't thievin'. Nobody can do anythin' to us.'

'Danneby might want to,' the other man muttered.

Strack snorted. 'He wouldn't know where to start lookin' for us. An' even if he did, there's four of us an' one of him. We got nothin' to worry about.'

'Except Vennor,' the third man said, 'drivin' us crazy with his whinin'.'

'We'll take him another bottle,' Strack growled. 'To shut him up.'

They all laughed, the sound of their voices fading as they went on down the path. And Elynne stood breathlessly still, hardly able to believe her luck.

Vennor had been left *alone*, at Strack's place — no doubt to guard the dragon's egg. So three of her enemies were out of the way, just like that.

Warily she moved back out to the path, then led Donnie on up the slope. In the woods a few birds chirped, a few flies buzzed, but everything remained peaceful. In a few minutes she was crouching behind a bush, looking at the robbers' hideout.

It was a small cabin made from rough planks, standing in a clearing, with a smelly outhouse nearby that made Elynne wrinkle her nose. The cabin door was facing her, and she could see a narrow, dirty window at one end.

All was silent, as if the cabin were deserted.

Then she heard a scraping thump from inside, followed by a muffled cough. She shrank back — but nothing happened, no one appeared, and silence fell once more. So she gathered her nerve, tied Donnie to a branch, and crept away.

She moved off through the woods, intending to circle around the clearing, unseen. As she went she was again feeling amazed, as she had that morning, amazed at where she had got to and what she was doing. And she was still winning the battle against her fear when she got far enough around the cabin to see that the other side of it was blank, with neither door nor window.

Without giving herself time to think about it, she flashed across the clearing, to crouch by the blank wall.

When her breathing and heartbeat had calmed down, she inched around the cabin until she was under the narrow window. Then she took several deep breaths and slowly raised herself up to peer in.

The interior of the one-room cabin was untidy and dirty, with a crude wooden bed and straw pallets on the floor for the other men. There was also an iron stove and other furniture, but Elynne's gaze fixed on a scarred table in the centre of the room. There Niys Vennor sat, a bottle in one hand – and a wooden box on the table in front of him.

Vennor seemed at least half-drunk, so Elynne

wondered hopefully whether he might fall asleep – until he suddenly lurched to his feet and stumbled towards the door. She dropped into a frozen crouch, ready to sprint for the safety of the woods. But Vennor didn't come around the cabin. She heard him staggering across the clearing, towards the outhouse.

Instantly, again before she knew she was going to do it, Elynne whisked around the cabin and in through the door.

Dashing to the table, she looked down into the lidless box. The egg was there, as she expected, gleaming rose-pink in the folds of a stained cloth. Eagerly she reached for it – but then paused as a thought struck her.

If she simply took it and ran, Vennor would discover its loss at once and quickly gather the other men to come after her. She needed a good head-start, to keep out of their clutches. And she knew just how to get it.

Struggling to keep her hands from shaking, she brought from her pocket the twist of paper holding some of her father's sleeping powders, and poured it into Vennor's bottle. Then she dived under the bed, holding her breath – partly because of the dirt and foul smells – and waited.

Before long Vennor stumbled back in, thumping down into his chair. Elynne heard him muttering to himself, then heard gurgling as he took a long drink. After that, his muttering grew more slurred, until at last his voice trailed away, and after a small thud he began to snore.

Peering cautiously out, she saw that Vennor had fallen face-forward on to the table. She sprang up, lifted the egg from the box, cradled it in her arms, and fled. Though she was careful not to fall with her precious burden, she took only seconds to get back to Donnie and untie him. She needed another moment to wrap her spare clothing and the blanket around the egg. Then she climbed on to Donnie's back, with the bundle in front of her, and headed back along the path towards the village.

She was smiling broadly, wanting to laugh with delight at how ridiculously easy it had all turned out to be. Coming out of the trees, turn-

ing along the village street, she was happily
imagining everyone's astonishment when she
arrived home with the rescued egg.

And then Strack and his two companions
stepped out of the tavern and into the street in
front of her.

Chapter Twelve

RUNNING HOME

Elynne went white with fear. But the men, taking her for one of the village children, didn't even look at her as they brushed past.

Sagging with relief, she urged Donnie to more speed. If the men were already on their way back to the cabin, they would discover their loss sooner than she had hoped. They might take a while to stir Vennor out of his drugged sleep, but they would be coming after her before long. She wanted to be as far away as possible by then.

Willing as ever, Donnie did his best. Soon they had left the village of Fallwood behind, rushing along the road towards the distant hills. Before too long, though it seemed like an age to

Elynne, the road began to rise in the first stage of its slope upwards towards the Slipstone Gap. The slope meant harder work for Donnie to keep up his pace. And by then long shadows were stretching out along the road, as the sun began to set.

Fright mounted within Elynne. As the afternoon waned, she would have given anything to get off the road and hide, as she had the night before. Yet there was no chance of that. As the road began to climb upwards, it also began to wind in among stony ridges and rock faces that closed in like the sides of a canyon. She could see no openings or paths that would lead away from the road.

At the same time, though, while Donnie laboured up the ever steeper, ever darker road, there was no sign of anyone behind them, riding out of Fallwood.

Of course the darkness and the winding road kept her from seeing very far behind – but she risked a brief halt now and then to listen, in silence, for the distant thunder of horses' hooves.

And she heard nothing at all, except a breeze sighing among the rocks and Donnie's soft panting.

Puzzled, she began hesitantly wondering if she really *was* being pursued. And finally she realised. The men would have no idea *who* had taken the egg, or which way that mysterious person would have gone. They might be searching in totally different directions, throughout the Greenbriar Valley. They might even have grown worried about being discovered, and decided to forget about the egg and flee.

Those cheering possibilities drove some of her fear away. Yet she still paused now and then to listen, just to be sure – and to let Donnie rest his weary legs that were crossing those rugged hills for the second time that day.

After several more ages, as it seemed, of endless tired plodding up the road's incline, both girl and donkey were startled to find that they had reached the crest of the Slipstone Gap. By then the moon was glimmering amid thin clouds – and its light showed the road behind them empty as far as Elynne could see.

Starting down the other side gave Donnie a small burst of new energy, so that they covered quite a distance over the next hour or so. That brought them far enough down the slope to be past the worst of the rocky walls on either side of the road. It also brought Elynne to such a state of late-night sleepiness that she worried she might fall off the donkey.

So, when the terrain allowed, they left the road – by means of a grassy gully that opened between tall ridges, then dipped down to make a small hollow, thick with brush, where a tiny fresh spring trickled from a stony crevice.

The exhausted donkey had a small drink and fell asleep almost instantly. But Elynne couldn't settle for the night without unwrapping the dragon egg and admiring it once more. Its pink colour looked pale in the moonlight filtering through the brush, but it was still a wondrous and beautiful thing. Trailing her fingertips over the egg's warm smoothness, she felt a pure and peaceful happiness, mixed in with a good deal of pride.

'You're safe now,' she whispered to the egg. 'You've been rescued. By *me*, little Lynnie. All by myself.'

Smiling, she began to wrap the egg up again. But then her heart leaped into her throat as a breath-stopping sound speared down into the vale.

Not any sort of human sound, but a monstrous shriek, far away yet still frightful – a raging challenge, tinged with over-tones of grief.

Elynne peered fearfully up through the brush at the moonlit, star-filled sky and saw the silhouette sweeping across that background, great wings wide-spread, soaring high over the ridges and the valley below. And she didn't need to see it more clearly, or to hear its second fierce echoing scream, to know what it was.

The Crimson Queen. Wheeling high above the land, crying out in the depths of her sorrow, mourning her loss.

But not just that, Elynne thought. She hasn't gone south, to the Cloudtower mountains, in the migration. She's still here. She's *searching*.

Elynne sank back on to her mossy bed, shivering. She had been so involved with all her own terrors and struggles, and then her escape with the egg, that she had almost forgotten about the Queen. She hadn't considered that the mother dragon might herself be searching for her egg.

The search would be hopeless for a wild dragon – but Elynne felt sure that the Queen would
not give up easily. And she had a very clear idea
of what would happen to anyone who had the
egg, if the Queen found them.

Before long the great red dragon swooped
away, her cries fading, so that Elynne fell at last
into an uneasy, dream-scarred sleep. But in what
seemed like no time at all she was dragged back
to wakefulness – by another unnerving sound.

A faint crackling, or crunching.

She sprang up fearfully, expecting to find the
robbers creeping up on her through the undergrowth. But she saw no one except Donnie,
blinking at her placidly. She also saw that the
sun was rising, so she had slept for longer than
she had imagined.

And then, finally, she realised where the sound
was coming from.

From the blanket-wrapped bundle containing
the egg.

Nervously she peeled away the wrappings –
and cried out with shock. The shiny, rosy sur-

face of the egg was *cracked*. Dozens of cracks, like thin dark scars, running in every direction. In a few places, small pieces of the shell had actually split off and fallen away.

It's broken, Elynne thought, horror-struck. Something must have happened to it in the night . . .

But then she heard another small crackling sound, and saw the egg move slightly as another tiny fragment of shell broke away. And the realisation struck her like a blow. The egg wasn't simply broken.

It was *hatching*.

Chapter Thirteen

LITTLE PRINCE

Ten minutes later, Elynne was face to face with a baby dragon. It – *he* – was about the size of a large bird, perhaps a hawk. And he looked a bit like a hawk, she thought, gazing warily at his bright yellow eyes and thorn-sharp claws, and the red-gold of his little scales.

But the fierce effect was lost when the baby took an unsteady step, nearly fell, then wobbled over to lean his head against her knee, looking up at her with a throaty cooing noise.

Carefully she reached down to stroke the red-gold head, marvelling at the glossy smoothness of the scales. And the baby wriggled with pleasure, cooing more loudly, his gaze filled with

unmistakeable love.

Elynne nearly laughed out loud, remembering that she had once seen exactly the same
thing happen with a duckling. It had become
attached to Aunt Pedda, because she was the first
living thing it had seen when it left the egg. The
duckling had only realised who its real mother
was when Pedda proved unwilling to swim
around in ponds.

Now, in the same way, the baby dragon thought Elynne was his mother.

The Crimson Queen wouldn't like this at all, she thought. But the Queen wasn't around, and the baby was very sweet. So she stroked him, and he cooed, and Donnie blinked at them with mild amazement.

'You need a name,' she murmured. 'And if your real mother is a Queen, you have to be . . . Prince.'

The little dragon looked startled by her voice. Then his own voice changed, and the cooing gave way to shrill, whimpering squeals.

Elynne smiled. 'Are you talking to me?'

It did seem that the dragon Prince was trying to say something. And as his squeals grew louder, Elynne realised what might be the trouble.

'You're probably *hungry!*' she said. 'Poor little Prince.'

She brought out her remaining scraps of food. Prince snapped eagerly at a bit of bread, then spat it out with a squeal, and did the same with a piece of dried fruit.

Dragons, Elynne reminded herself, eat *meat*. And she hadn't brought any.

'You'll have to wait,' she told Prince, petting him. 'You'll get lots of meat when we get home.'

Being petted turned Prince's squeals back into cooing, for a moment. But his shrill cries began again, insistently, while Elynne gathered her things and climbed on to Donnie's back with the little dragon tucked in one arm. Untroubled by the noisy new passenger, Donnie obediently set off along the gully that led back to the road. And Elynne kept petting Prince soothingly, which quietened his cries.

Shortly she was very glad of that. She was also glad that she had had the sense to pause behind a screen of briars growing by the mouth of the gully, to be sure that the way was clear and the road was safe. Hidden there, with Prince silent, she heard the stamp of horses' hooves on the road. And then heard – with an icy clutch of fright – the deep, rough voice of the man named Strack.

'Maybe it wasn't the Danneby brat, after all,'

Strack was growling. 'We've seen no sign of her.'

'I dunno,' said the sour voice of Niys Vennor. 'They said in the village that a girl went up to the cabin with a donkey. It's got to be Danneby's girl.' He spat angrily. 'Must've been someone with her. That little weak-knee couldn't do nothin' on her own.'

'Maybe they went another way,' another voice suggested.

Strack grunted. 'We'll keep on this way awhile, since we've come this far. But whichever way they went, we'll get 'em. I promise you that. We'll make 'em sorry they was ever born, for givin' us all this trouble.'

The brutal menace of those words made Elynne shiver. But despite that, she nudged Donnie forward, one quiet step, so that she could see the road.

The four robbers had dismounted from their horses, and one of them was probing with a knife at his horse's hoof as if prying a stone from the shoe. As she watched, that man nodded, put the knife away, and they all mounted again and rode off. Westward – in the direction of Elynne's home.

She stayed in the gully for some while after their sounds had died away, again battling against fright, trying to think clearly. If she went on homeward, the robbers could be waiting for her. Yet she not only wanted, achingly, to go home – she *needed* to go home. Because she had a hungry baby dragon in her care.

As if on cue, Prince began squirming again, with another burst of shrill crying. Elynne fervently hoped that the robbers were far enough away not to hear those squeals – especially because, by then, the baby's hunger pangs were too great to be soothed by petting. And suddenly, weirdly, as Donnie moved forward towards the road, Prince's cries seemed to be echoed – by a distant, terrifying scream.

Donnie's head jerked up, ears quivering. And Elynne stared up as well, with new terror squeezing the breath from her lungs.

Swooping above the nearest mountain ridge, a blood-red streak against the morning sky, was the Crimson Queen.

Quickly Elynne jerked at the reins, turning the frightened donkey back towards the gully. Both were entirely silent, breathless with terror. But the baby dragon, unaware of anything but his own hunger, squealed the loudest, shrillest squeal of all, struggling wildly in Elynne's grip.

They hadn't quite reached the mouth of the gully when Prince twisted free of Elynne's hands – fluttering down to the ground, with another piercing squeal.

And high above them, drawn by the sound, the Crimson Queen swerved in her flight, hurtling like a giant red spear towards the roadside where Elynne was cowering.

Chapter Fourteen

NARROW ESCAPES

E lynne went rigid with terror – but Donnie, by instinct, galloped frantically forwards. In just a few strides he and Elynne were back among the briars in the gully. And in that moment, from somewhere on the ground, Prince's shrill squeals abruptly cut off.

Elynne looked down – to see the little dragon silently stalking a toad that squatted in the briars' shade. As she looked, he pounced, snatching up the toad and devouring it in two gulps.

In that instant, the Crimson Queen flashed past overhead, not looking in their direction, unaware of their presence now that Prince's cries had stopped. And Prince, looking pleased with

himself as he readily returned to Elynne, also failed to see the huge crimson dragon circling high above them before disappointedly soaring away.

Weak with relief, Elynne gathered Prince up and guided Donnie back to the road again. And when both the road ahead and the sky above remained quiet and empty, she was able to relax a little while Donnie trotted along, and Prince dozed contentedly in her arms. Strack and the others would be a long way ahead by then, she thought. And with luck, when they found she wasn't at home, they would simply go away and search elsewhere.

So the day drifted by, the road wound on, and nothing unusual happened. They left the road briefly around midday, to give Donnie a rest and to find a clear little stream to give them all a drink. There Elynne finished the last of her food while Prince found a cluster of fat caterpillars that seemed to please him.

Then they rode on, past fields and woods drowsing in the sun, still undisturbed. And finally they came to the top of a low rise and saw the village of Lowfield in the distance.

Quickly Elynne moved Donnie backwards, below the rise – because it occurred to her that the robbers might have stopped in Lowfield. Anyway, she wasn't about to ride through the village carrying a baby dragon, who was getting hungry again, squirming and squealing.

So once again she turned Donnie off the road, into the fields behind Lowfield, where trees and bushes offered useful cover. To be safe she also wrapped Prince in her blanket, covering him completely.

The darkness and the warmth soothed him, and he grew quiet. Relieved, Elynne dismounted and began a stealthy detour around the village. Creeping through a copse of trees fairly near one of the village's clusters of cottages, carrying Prince and leading Donnie, she was peering cautiously around in every direction – except downward. So she failed to see the gnarled tree root jutting up in her path.

Her foot caught it, she sprawled, and the

blanket-wrapped Prince slipped from her grasp. Before she could get to him, the little dragon fought free of the blanket and fluttered off into the wood, squealing.

In panic, Elynne dashed after him – but the greenery seemed to swallow him up. As she frantically searched, she could hear his shrill squeals here and there in the wood. But when she rushed in those directions, there was no sign of him.

After several more minutes, she heard the squeals again. Combined with the terrified squawking of chickens, and a man's angry yell.

'Somethin's after the *hens!*' he yelled. 'Where's my gun?'

Elynne sprinted towards the sounds, almost sobbing with desperation. Reaching the edge of the wood, she skidded to a halt. Ahead she saw a large yard belonging to a small neat cottage – a yard with a vegetable garden and a hen-house, where a red-faced man carrying a rusty musket was stalking around, glaring. And no sign of Prince.

But at the same time, beyond the cottage, she

glimpsed a part of Lowfield's main road. Where she saw four men, idling in front of the village tavern: Strack, Vennor and the others.

Dodging back among the trees, she almost screamed at a touch on her leg. Looking down, she saw Prince, again seeming pleased with himself. With something suspiciously like a chicken-feather caught on the scales by his nose.

Scooping him up, she fled back to Donnie. In another moment they were hurrying away through the wood and the fields beyond it, with Prince once again wrapped securely in the blanket, leaving the village and the robbers behind.

Before long they were out of sight of Lowfield, able to return to the road – once she was sure it was clear. And when at last they began that last lap of the journey, despite all her anxiety a huge shining excitement built up within Elynne.

She constantly looked back, of course, watching for pursuit – but she was also looking forward, to arriving home with her sensational surprise. By then, after his adventures and the food, the surprise himself was sound asleep in the blanket. But Donnie seemed to share her excitement, knowing they were nearly home, for his ears were pointed eagerly forwards and he was trotting at an impressive pace.

At last, with the mid-afternoon sun easing itself towards the western sky, they rode into the farmstead yard under the 'Dragon Charmer' sign. If there had been anybody about to see her arrival, she might have yelled a greeting, full of the joy and triumph bubbling up inside her. But the yard was empty, the house silent.

Quickly she slid down from Donnie's back, leading him into the paddock, neatly hanging up the bridle. And then, with Prince still asleep in the blanket, she carried her bundle into the house.

And created total uproar.

Chapter Fifteen

TRIUMPH & TERROR

When Elynne walked calmly into the kitchen, Aunt Pedda's firm briskness vanished. She went white, dropped a bowl to smash on the floor, and shrieked, 'Lynnie', before clutching Elynne in a frantic hug, despite the bulk of the bundle. With all of that the bundle stirred slightly, but Pedda didn't notice. She was too busy hugging Elynne and demanding to know where she had been and scolding her all at once.

Then they rushed to Dan's room – where Elynne was thrilled to see her father sitting up in bed, chatting with Old Gidge, looking more like himself despite some paleness and the heavy bandages around his head, arm and ribs.

Both men shouted with surprise and delight when they saw her – and then Dan also began to scold and question her while trying to hug her, one-armed, past the awkward bundle. Which again moved a little, still unnoticed.

But after they had all calmed down, and after Elynne had told them over and over that she was perfectly all right, the three adults gazed at her curiously. Normally, whenever she received even the mildest of scoldings, Elynne would cringe and droop and perhaps even weep. But now . . . she was just standing there calmly, holding her bundle, and smiling – an odd, *secret* sort of smile.

'I'm sorry that I worried you . . .' she began.

'You certainly did that,' Pedda said, regaining some of her briskness.

'Thought you'd been kidnapped or some-thin',' Old Gidge cackled.

'Why, Lynnie?' Dan asked insistently. 'Why did you go off like that?'

Elynne's face grew serious. 'I had to. Because

[121]

. . . all those terrible things that happened, the egg being stolen, you being hurt – they were sort of my fault. I mean, I might have kept it from happening.'

'But no one was blaming *you*, child,' Pedda said.

'Is that why you ran off, Lynnie?' her father asked gently. 'Because you thought we'd blame you?'

'No, no,' Elynne said quickly. 'I went because I thought – from something Strack said – that I knew where they'd *gone*, with the egg. And I wanted to get it back. To make everything better again.'

The three of them gaped at her.

'*You?*' Pedda cried. 'Little Lynnie? You went chasing after the thieves all by *yourself?*'

'I had to,' Elynne said again, quietly. 'There wasn't anyone else. I had to try.'

The three adults went silent, still staring at her – noting how she met their gaze with a clear-eyed calm, how she stood straight and still as she faced them.

'Well, well,' her father said at last, smiling. 'You found some courage from somewhere, all at once, didn't you?'

'It's what you told me,' she reminded him. 'You said if someone wants something badly enough, they stop being afraid.'

'Two nights away from home by yourself,' Aunt Pedda grumbled. 'That's a little too much courage to find, at your age, if you ask me.'

But Dan shifted his gaze to peer hopefully at the bundle in Elynne's arms. 'So what happened, Lynnie? Did you find the men, with the egg? Is . . . is that it?'

Elynne's secret smile reappeared. 'No,' she told them. 'This is better.'

She unwrapped the blanket. And the three adults went as still as statues, mouths hanging open, stunned by the sight of the little red-gold dragon. Who blinked at them, then showed all of his sharp little teeth in a sleepy yawn.

'Good heavens,' Dan breathed. 'It hatched.'

'His name's Prince, of course,' Elynne went on. 'And he's very tame. He thinks I'm his mother.'

'Amazin',' Gidge whispered.

'I think our Lynnie is what's amazing,' Dan said proudly. 'What a fantastic adventure! Had the egg hatched before you found the robbers?'

'No,' Elynne began, 'it was still an egg when I stole it back. They were . . .'

'Wait, wait, now,' Pedda interrupted. 'These robbers – just where are *they*, right now? Do they know it was you that took the egg?'

Elynne looked shocked. 'Oh – yes! I should've said! They do think it was me, and they were in Lowfield!'

'Then they'll be on their way here,' Dan said grimly. 'Gidge, maybe you should go and watch the road. If you spot them before they get here, we'll have time to get Lynnie and Prince safely hidden somewhere.'

'They could come after dark,' Pedda pointed out – and Elynne looked at the window, half-open in the day's warmth, seeing that the sun was settling westward, beginning to lengthen the shadows.

'Don't matter,' Gidge said determinedly. 'I'll

see 'em or hear 'em.'

As he hurried away, Elynne glanced nervously away from the window towards the flimsy bedroom door. 'Maybe we should all leave,' she said tensely. 'There're four of them!'

'We can't go anywhere,' Pedda reminded her. 'The doctor said your father had to stay still while his head healed.'

'Don't worry,' Dan said confidently. 'They won't be interested in us – and we can send them on a false trail, then maybe send some constables after them.' He looked again at Prince, snuggling in Elynne's arms, who yawned again and rubbed his head lovingly against her shoulder. 'Meanwhile, I want to hear all about how you stole the egg back, and then we can work out what to do with your little friend there.'

Elynne sighed shakily. 'I wish we could keep him. But he's the Crimson Queen's baby – and she's still around, looking for him. I saw her, twice.'

'Is she?' Dan asked interestedly. 'You're right, she ought to have her baby back. But first I'd really like to see how Prince might respond to the pipes . . .'

Before he could go on, the door to the bed-room crashed open, and Old Gidge stumbled in, almost falling, as if he had been roughly pushed from behind.

And in his wake came Strack and Vennor and the other two men – gripping ugly cudgels and knives in their hands, peering with amazement at the little dragon.

'You won't be playin' any pipes with that thing,' Strack growled. 'It's *ours*.'

Chapter Sixteen

PRINCE IN FLIGHT

Elynne and the others were motionless, as if paralysed, as the men crowded in. And Gidge, slumping in a chair, looked sadly at Dan.

'Sorry, Dan,' he mumbled. 'They jumped me in the yard. . .'

Dan stirred as if about to lunge out of bed to confront the men, before Pedda gripped his arm.

'Don't, Dan!' she said quickly. 'You mustn't get up!'

Strack grinned. 'Do like she says, friend, or you'll need more bandages.'

'What happened to you, Danneby?' Vennor chortled. 'The big red dragon bite you?' Then he frowned, puzzled, as a thought occurred to him.

'Here – if you've been hurt, who was it came after us, with little Miss Mousy?'

Elynne stiffened, her rage at the traitorous Vennor boiling up, sweeping fear aside. 'There was no one with me!' she cried. 'I did it by myself!'

'Oh, yeah,' Vennor sneered. 'Tell us another one.'

'Leave it, Vennor,' Strack rumbled. 'Get the little dragon.' He grinned his cruel grin again. 'It'll be worth *ten times* what we would've got for the egg.'

Vennor glowered as Elynne drew back. 'Hand it over,' he snarled, 'or you'll be sorry.'

As he reached for her, Elynne tried to dodge aside, but Vennor was too quick. Clamping one bony hand on her shoulder, he reached for Prince with the other.

But the little dragon had a wild creature's reflexes. When he saw a threatening stranger clutching at him, he reacted – by sinking his sharp little fangs into Vennor's hand.

As Vennor howled and jerked away, Prince tore himself from Elynne's grasp, and disappeared in a fluttering dive through the half-open window.

'Prince!' Elynne cried desperately.

'Get after it!' Strack roared.

'My hand – I'm bleedin',' Vennor whimpered.

Strack clutched the front of his shirt furiously. 'You'll have more'n that to cry about if we don't find that dragon!'

'It could go anywhere,' one of the others grumbled.

'Then get *movin'*!' Strack bellowed, and wheeled back to Vennor. 'If you're hurtin' so much, stay here an' watch this lot, keep 'em out of our way!'

He and the others stormed out, leaving a tense and angry silence in the room.

Scowling, Vennor snatched a roll of Dan's bandages, then backed towards the door to bind up his injured hand. And Elynne, watching him, was thinking quickly. There was an iron bolt on the inside of the door – which was giving her an idea.

She put on her most innocent expression. 'I don't think Prince will get lost,' she said brightly to Dan. 'He's run off before, but he always comes back to me.'

Dan nodded vaguely, glowering at Vennor.

'Most times he comes back in just a minute or two,' Elynne went on, still looking innocent. 'He's never been alone much . . .' As she spoke, she moved her gaze towards the doorway behind Vennor, and opened her eyes wide. 'Oh, look, look!' she cried, pointing. 'There he is!'

The trick worked perfectly. Startled, Vennor whirled and charged into the hall beyond the doorway, ready to pounce. And instantly Elynne slammed the door behind him, crashing the bolt home. Then, before anyone else could move or speak, she darted across the room and plunged headfirst out through the window.

Landing in a tumble, she leaped up and raced away, unseen by Strack and the other two men who were crashing around at the other end of the house. And as she ran, she was once again thinking quickly.

Dragons are winged creatures, she was thinking, and mountain creatures. So Prince, by nature, might look for a refuge up on something *high*. And the highest thing around there was the barn.

The big building's main doors stood slightly open. Creeping in, Elynne paused while her eyes grew used to the dimness, then peered around. There was an open area in the centre of the barn, with stalls for horses along either side. There was also a mass of harness, farm equipment and tools along the walls, and a hayloft above, reached by a ladder. But no sign of Prince.

Tilting her head, she listened intently. Was that a faint scratching somewhere? And was it mice – or a small, frightened dragon?

In a low murmur she called Prince's name. And a rush of relief and joy poured through her as she heard the little dragon's soft cooing reply, coming from above her. In the dragon manner, Prince had found a hiding place well off the ground – in the hayloft.

Scrambling up the ladder, she peered around at the bales of hay and the tightly closed hayloft door before calling again. And she nearly fell out of the loft when Prince's head again unex-pectedly bumped against her side.

Gathering him up, cuddling him as he cooed in her arms, she clambered back down the lad-der and started towards the door. But then she jerked to a halt, her heart seeming to stop.

Outside, terrifyingly close, she heard Strack's growling voice.

'The barn's got lots of places to hide,' he was growling. 'Keep your eyes open.'

Panic flooded through Elynne as she heard their heavy tread almost at the door. But she fought the panic with all her strength, and leaped back towards the ladder.

Quickly she rushed up again, with Prince wriggling nervously in her arms. Then, though its weight was almost too much for her, she struggled to drag the ladder up with her. After that, panting and frightened, but determined, she looked around for the long, two-pronged hay-fork.

And finally, as the men stamped in below, she crouched behind a hay bale, with the hay-fork beside her, hugging Prince close. And waited.

Chapter Seventeen

FINAL FURY

'It'll take us till dark to look all through this place,' she heard Vennor complain.

'It'd better not,' Strack growled. 'If we lose that little dragon because you let the girl trick you, Vennor, you'll wish you'd never been born!'

'It wasn't . . .' Vennor began to whine. But then he stopped. 'Here!' he said, his voice rising. 'The *ladder's* gone!'

Strack understood at once. 'Yeah – the loft,' he said thoughtfully. He raised his voice. 'If you're up there with that dragon, girlie, you better come on down!'

Behind her bale of hay, Elynne quivered slightly, remaining silent. But Prince – sensing her fear and the threat in the man's voice – squeaked with nervous shrillness before she could stop him.

The men below laughed roughly. 'Dragon's up there, for sure,' one said.

'An' it didn't pull up the ladder,' Strack growled, then raised his voice again. 'Come on, girl – if we have to come an' get you, you'll be sorry!'

Anger boiled up in Elynne again, breaking through her frightened silence. 'You just go away!' she shouted. 'You're not getting him!'

'That's the only ladder on the place,' Vennor was saying sourly. 'How do we get up there?'

'Get some wood,' one of the others said. 'Make another ladder.'

'If you try to come up here,' Elynne yelled, 'I'll put Prince out through the hayloft door! You'll *never* catch him!'

She had no real wish to do that, since it would be like abandoning the baby dragon to his fate – and anyway, Prince would probably just come back to her as always. But the men took her threat seriously.

'We got to stop her!' Vennor was snarling. 'The thing could fly off anywhere!'

'Forget it,' Strack rumbled. 'I've got an idea.'

They moved away towards the barn door, lowering their voices so that Elynne couldn't hear their words. Then everything went quiet. After some minutes she gathered enough nerve to creep forward, clutching Prince, and peer over the edge of the loft.

Vennor and one of the strangers lounged by the barn door. But then she heard voices outside – and went limp and icy with horror.

Pedda and Gidge, supporting Dan between them, were being pushed into the barn by Strack and the fourth man.

'Right, girlie!' Strack's voice rose in a roar. 'Come down an' join the party!'

Quivering, Elynne watched the four men form a circle around their prisoners, with cudgels and knives held menacingly. Pedda and Gidge were pale with fright, while Dan – pale with the pain of being moved – still glared with fearless anger.

'Listen good, now, girlie!' Strack was growling. 'You put the ladder back an' bring the little dragon down, right now – or your folks will get a bashin'!'

As Vennor snickered evilly, Elynne sagged. She no longer had any choices.No matter what nasty plans the men might have for Prince, she could never allow them to harm her father and the others.

'All right,' she said dully. 'I'm coming down.' She wrestled with the ladder, while keeping a firm hold on the struggling Prince. As the ladder slid down with a crash, it was seized and slammed firmly into place. And before she could start down, someone came clambering swiftly up.

Niys Vennor – who stopped at the top of the ladder, scowling at her.

'I ain't lettin' you try any more tricks,' he snarled. 'Gimme that beast, now.'

Again, wild rage flared in Elynne. Again, she reacted without thinking, without knowing she was going to do anything.

'No!' she screamed. And she snatched up the hay-fork, and jabbed its glittering prongs at Vennor.

In the same instant, Prince added his voice and his rage to hers, with a shrill, fierce dragon-shriek that seemed to fill the barn.

Vennor jerked back, wide-eyed with shock, and his foot slipped. With a howl he toppled backwards off the ladder, crashing to the ground, where he lay still before starting to wriggle slowly.

The other men scarcely looked at him. 'Come on, girl,' Strack rumbled, raising his heavy cudgel. 'I'm waitin'.'

At the foot of the ladder Vennor slowly heaved himself up, one arm hanging limply. 'I think I bust a collarbone,' he whined.

Still everyone ignored him as they watched Elynne climb slowly down the ladder, with Prince tucked in one arm. On the ground, her eyes glazed with misery, she stepped around the moaning Vennor and backed away as Strack started towards her.

'You let them go, first,' she quavered. 'You don't get Prince till you do.'

'I'll get him *now*,' Strack growled. 'C'mere!'

He lunged forward, and Elynne cried out, leaping away, as Prince screamed again with another shrill challenge.

But then all sounds were silenced, all movements halted. Around them the entire barn was shaken, while above them a huge portion of the roof's stout tiles and rafters were ripped away as if they were tissue paper. By a shrieking, raging, demonic, unstoppable force.

The Crimson Queen.

Staggered by the sudden eruption of terrible noise and power, Elynne saw every detail of what happened next with perfect clarity, as if in slow motion.

She saw the Queen's great body blast in through the opening she had made, wings spread, talons outstretched.

She saw Strack's other two men wheel in terror and gallop wildly out of the barn – while Pedda and Gidge staggered back towards the door with Dan, also trying to escape the monstrous, plunging descent of the dragon.

She saw a mass of broken tiles and wood, torn from the barn's roof, fall with deadly accuracy directly on top of Strack. Leaving him stunned on the floor, half-buried.

She saw the Queen swoop to a landing in the

middle of the barn, lashing out with a huge leathery wing to sweep Vennor out of her way, hurling him across the barn to lie crumpled and still.

Finally, with Prince silent and astonished in her arms, she saw that the mighty dragon had landed between her and the doorway.

And the Queen was advancing towards her, terrible fangs bared, huge eyes burning like molten gold.

Chapter Eighteen

DRAGON SONG

Total, quivering, terror-filled silence descended on the barn. Even the huge crimson dragon herself was soundless in her slow advance, her savage glare almost hypnotic as it fixed unblinkingly on the little girl holding the little dragon.

Step by numb step, Elynne backed away – until she reached the wall of the barn, and could go no farther. With the Queen looming before her, eyes ablaze, fangs and claws glinting.

'Help me,' Elynne said in a whisper that was almost a sob.

Across the barn, still supported by Pedda and Gidge, Dan gave a choked cry and lurched forward. But he was too weak from his wounds, and might have fallen if Pedda and Gidge had not grasped him again. And the dragon-pipes that might have stopped the Queen were back in the house.

And so, with no possible help coming from anywhere else, Elynne began instinctively to help herself.

Stiffly, half-stupefied by the Queen's molten eyes, she placed the little Prince on the ground in front of her. The Queen's dreadful gaze shifted, to focus on her baby. And Prince, staring up at the huge red creature towering above him, moved nervously back to Elynne for reassurance.

Automatically, responding as so often before to the little dragon's nervousness, Elynne reached down to stroke him.

'Go on,' she murmured tremulously. 'That's your real mother. That's who you belong with.'

Watching, the Queen halted her menacing advance. Though she could hardly have understood all that had happened, she could see that her baby was not in any danger. She also seemed to sense the loving warmth of the bond that existed between the human child and her own.

The fury faded from her golden eyes, her flared wings lowered. Stretching her neck down towards Prince, she began a rich crooning, deep in her throat.

Prince's eyes widened. Slowly he took a step away from Elynne, then another. Hesitantly, he replied – with the high sweet cooing that Elynne knew so well.

Elynne's eyes grew moist as she saw her little Prince moving away towards his true mother. And then, as the two dragons crooned and cooed, she began – for reasons that she would never fully understand – to hum softly, joining in their music.

Slowly her voice rose into a wordless song, clear and pure. As it rose, the dragons' voices faded and fell silent. And her father and the others, across the barn, stared with disbelief.

Elynne was singing the dragon – charming music. And, just as if it were coming from the pipes, it was taking effect.

The Queen's neck arched, her body relaxed, her eyes half-closed. Slowly, dreamily, the huge creature began the soft, deep humming of the tranced dragon. Then, as Elynne's voice lifted and the song went on, she began the sinuous graceful swaying, the slow delicate movements, lost in her trance.

And just as dreamily, just as lost in a trance although it was his first time, the little Prince swayed and moved beside his mother. Together, in perfect unison, mirroring each other's every curve and step and bend.

Still singing, Elynne edged forward, circling around the tranced dragons, who slowly turned to face her as she went. Still singing, she backed away towards her father, while the dragons swayed and hummed in their eerie togetherness. Still singing, she kept moving, with the other three, until they reached the doorway.

'All right, Lynnie,' her father said quietly.

She let the song trail away to an end. For a moment, as the dragons subsided, they remained motionless, eyes still half-shut. Then the Queen awoke from the last of her trance, hissing softly as her eyes opened.

For a long breathless moment they stared at one another, the people and the dragons – before the Queen picked the Prince up in her forelimbs, spread mighty wings, and leaped up and out through the ruined roof.

Elynne sighed, a tear trickling down her cheek as they heard the rush of dragon-wings fading high above them. Then her father put his good arm around her in a fierce hug.

'That *song*,' he said to her, his voice filled with wonder. 'How did you do it?'

'I don't know,' Elynne whispered. 'It just came.'

'But no one has *ever* done dragon charming without the pipes!' Dan said.

'Someone has now,' Old Gidge said merrily.

'I never could play the pipes very well anyway,' Elynne murmured.

Aunt Pedda peered at her. 'You couldn't do *lots* of things, before,' she said. 'Seems you're like a whole new person!'

Dan grinned, hugging Elynne close. 'It's how people change, I suppose. By finding out what they're really able to do – when it needs to be done.'

'I was still afraid, though,' Elynne told him. 'All the time.'

'That's what being brave is,' he said gently.

'Doing what needs doing despite being afraid.'

'And you surely did it, child,' Pedda said, smiling. 'All by yourself – saved the day, protected your Prince, defeated the villains. You can be *proud!*'

'I just feel sad,' Elynne said, her voice catching. 'I didn't want to lose Prince.'

'He's where he belongs, Lynnie,' her father said.

'An' I'm gettin' me some rope an' tie up Vennor an' that Strack,' Gidge said. 'Then the constable can come take 'em where *they* belong – jail!'

'And you can go back to bed where *you* belong, Dan Danneby,' Pedda said briskly. 'Before you do yourself any more damage.'

'I'm all right,' Dan assured her. 'I just hurt a bit. No harm done.' He smiled at Elynne. 'And I have a feeling that we'll see the Prince and the Queen again – starting with the spring migration, when the dragons fly north. My feeling says that the Queen will bring her baby back here, with the others.'

'That'll bring the crowds to the show!' Gidge cackled. 'Especially with Lynnie singin' in it!'

Elynne's eyes went wide. 'In the *show?*' she breathed. 'Do you think I could?'

Dan's smile widened. 'I think, now, you could do just about anything that you really want to do.'

'You've found your courage, love,' Pedda put in. 'It's not going to go away.'

'That's right,' Dan said firmly, smiling. 'You can stay back at the edge of the basin, at first – but I don't think you'll ever be so afraid of dragons again, Lynnie, after all this. I'm absolutely sure that you can do it. And when you're older, and more sure of yourself, you can come and walk among them with me.'

Elynne just looked at him, starry-eyed and speechless.

'With a show like that,' Gidge said gleefully, 'we'll get rich!'

'We could do with some richness now,' Pedda said. 'To pay for mending that barn roof.'

Dan laughed. 'We can afford it. But even

before that, we're going to have to make a new sign. From now on, up over the gate, it's going to say:

'DANNEBY AND _DAUGHTER_ – DRAGON CHARMERS.'

About the author

Douglas Hill was born in Canada but now lives in North London. Over the years Douglas worked at many jobs but finally settled for being a journalist and writer, for both adults and children. Best known for his large output of science fiction, including the successful *Warriors of in the Wasteland* trilogy (Pan Macmillan), Douglas also enjoys forays into fantasy.

Some other Barn Owls you may enjoy

PRIVATE — KEEP OUT!
by Gwen Grant

The hilarious adventures of a girl, the youngest of six, growing up in a mining town just after World War II. Our heroine, high spirited, impulsive, stubborn, is never out of trouble but always manages to remain lovable.

Written in the first person, this is a lovely funny book that also gives a great picture of England recovering from the War.

STRANGE EXCHANGE
by Pat Thomson

Mike has a real shock when he discovers that his French exchange student is in fact an alien, come to find out about humans and life on earth. When the *real* French student turns up things get very complicated. But Mum and Dad can cope — I mean everyone knows that foreigners are mad!

"Excellent wit and humour. Had me laughing out loud."
Chris Stevenson, *The Observer*

THE MUSTANG MACHINE
by Chris Powling

The Mustang Machine is a magical bike, whoever owns it will be faster than anyone else. That makes it absolutely vital that the machine does not fall into the wrong hands. One way or another Tim and his friends have to stop Dennis the Bully claiming the bike as his own.

A very entertaining story about dealing with bullies and playing fair at the same time.

VLAD THE DRAC
by Ann Jungman

When Judy and Paul find a baby vampire in Romania, they take him home as a souvenir. Vlad the Drac is unlike other vampires . . . He may be a vegetarian who faints at the sight of blood, but Judy and Paul still have to keep him a secret. Vlad gets them into all kinds of trouble, expecially as he loves a little attention. Then one day Vlad can remain a secret no longer . . .

"These stories are excellent for young readers." Nicholas Tucker, The Rough Guide to Children's Books

VLAD THE DRAC RETURNS
by Ann Jungman

Vlad the Drac, the diminutive vegetarian vampire is back in London, to attend the première of a new vampire film. Now that he is famous for his flights round Count Dracula's castle, Vlad has no intention of slumming it with his friends the Stones, So he plans to stay at the Ritz. As always with Vlad, nothing works out as planned and the Stone family are plunged into another series of anarchic, hilarious adventures.

"Funny, unpredictable, playful and defiant, Vlad is always excellent company." Nicholas Tucker, The Rough Guide to Children's Books

YOU'RE THINKING ABOUT DOUGHNUTS
by Michael Rosen

When Frank has to spend an evening on his own at the museum he is both scared and bored. But then a skeleton comes alive and takes Frank on a most unusual tour of the museum's exhibits and the time flies past.

Michael Rosen at his hilarious, sparkling best!

LIAR, LIAR, PANTS ON FIRE!
by Jeremy Strong

Susie Bonner is a town girl right down to the tips of her toes but mum has decided to move to the country and life in a small place is not to Susie's taste. To keep up her spirits Susie writes regularly to her best friend Marsha with an account of her new life but Susie has a vivid imagination and can't help adding drama to her letters. So when Marsha comes to stay and sees village life as it really is, things get a bit difficult!

An amusing, perceptive tale from the master of comedy Jeremy Strong.

"Guaranteed entertainment." Lindsay Fraser in the *Glasgow Herald*.

THE BLOOD AND THUNDER ADVENTURE ON HURRICANE PEAK
by Margaret Mahy

One of Margaret Mahy's wonderful, chaotic, zany, fantastic stories. In the great city of Hookywalker lives wicked Sir Quincey Judd-Sprockett in his super modern wheelchair. Sir Quincey is determined to close down the Unexpected School on Hurricane Peak, where young Huxley and Zara Hammond have been sent by their parents. The school is full of unusual characters, Heathcliff Warlock the magical school teacher, Zanzibar the feline head prefect and the amazing inventor Belladonna Doppler. Will this unlikely crew manage to foil the fiendish Sir Quincey? Of course they will and loads of fun on the way.